Lulu Frost is the pen name of Angela McAllister, who has written over sixty books for children of all ages, including several award winners. She lives with her family in an old cottage in Hampshire, England, hoping one day to see a fairy in her yard.

Lorna Brown studied fine art painting in college and works as an artist and illustrator from her cottage in Somerset, England. Lorna also works as an animal therapist, so she has the perfect balance between art and her love of animals and the outdoors!

Fran Brylewska studied animation at art college, where she met her husband David. After illustrating children's pre-school magazines, Fran formed her own illustration company with David in 1997. They now work and live in Dorset, England, with their children Zac and Anya.

This edition published by Parragon Books Ltd in 2016 and distributed by

Parragon Inc.
440 Park Avenue South, 13th Floor
New York, NY 10016
www.parragon.com

Please retain this information for future reference.

Written by Lulu Frost
Edited by Laura Baker
Illustrated by Lorna Brown and Fran Brylewska
Production by Jonathan Wakeham

ISBN 978-1-4454-9891-1

Printed in China

The Moonlight Tooth Fairy

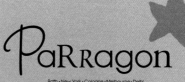

Bath · New York · Cologne · Melbourne · Delhi
Hong Kong · Shenzhen · Singapore

Twinkle was a tooth fairy.

Every night, she flew from house to house collecting the teeth that children had left under their pillows.

Each time she took a tooth, she slipped a shiny coin in its place.

Before she flew away,
she always whispered,
"Sweet dreams!"

Twinkle loved to make
people happy.

But Twinkle often felt lonely.
She saw sisters sharing a bedroom.

She saw friends sleeping over.

She saw moonlit moths
playing together.

"I wish I had a friend, too," she thought.

One night Twinkle came to Abigail's house. She flew in the open window and tiptoed onto Abigail's pillow.

Carefully,
Twinkle reached
for Abigail's
tooth and put
it in her tooth
fairy pouch.

She pulled
out a shiny coin ...

But suddenly Twinkle felt that somebody was watching her. Slowly she turned around.
A fairy face was staring at her in the moonlight!

"Silly me," thought Twinkle. "It's only a picture!" Then she noticed that there were fairies everywhere! Twinkle was so amazed that she didn't look where she was flying ...

Ouch! Twinkle bumped into a bookshelf and dropped the coin. It clattered onto the floor and rolled behind the cupboard. The noise woke Abigail.

Twinkle knew that the Tooth Fairy should never be seen.

With a flit of her wings, she darted behind the curtain.

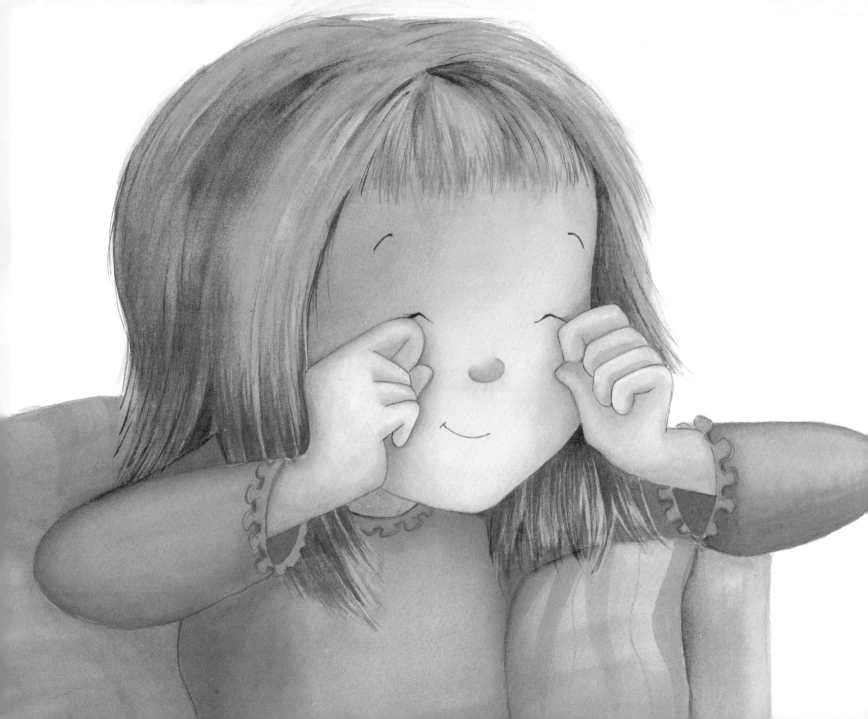

Abigail sat up in bed and rubbed her sleepy eyes.

Twinkle peeped out from behind the curtain. She watched Abigail put her hand under her pillow. The tooth was gone, but there was nothing in its place!

"Poor Abigail," thought Twinkle. "If only I had another coin." But her pouch was empty.

Abigail's eyes filled with tears. "Maybe the tooth fairy thinks I haven't been good," she said.

"Oh no!" Twinkle cried out. "That's not true!"

Abigail spotted Twinkle and gasped with amazement.

"Oh dear," thought Twinkle. "Now I've broken the Tooth Fairy Rule!"

Twinkle knew she had been seen, so she fluttered over to the bed.
She gave Abigail her tiny hankie.

"I'm sorry, Abigail," she whispered.
"I lost your coin."

Abigail gazed at the moonlight
glistening on the fairy's silvery wings
and smiled.

"Am I dreaming?" she asked.

"No, you're not dreaming!"
laughed Twinkle.

Twinkle explained what had happened. She watched Abigail gazing at her wings and had an idea. "Would you like me to give you a wish instead of a coin?" she asked.

Abigail's eyes sparkled with excitement. "Oh, yes please! There's something that I've always wished for," she said shyly.

"Yes?" asked Twinkle.

"I wish to be a fairy, just like you!"

Twinkle waved magic
into the room.

Suddenly Abigail felt herself shrinking.
Her pajamas turned into a beautiful dress
made of petals, and little rosebuds blossomed
in her hair. Something tickled her shoulders ...

"Look!" she cried. "I'm growing wings!"
Sure enough, Abigail was soon as tiny
as Twinkle, with a matching pair of
shimmery wings.

Gently Abigail opened her wings and gave them a flutter.
"Will you teach me how to fly?" she asked.
"It's easy!" said Twinkle. "Hold my hand ..."

And up they rose!

Twinkle and Abigail flew to the mirror
so Abigail could admire her new wings.
Then Twinkle led Abigail out into the
moonlit yard.

Twinkle and Abigail
flew high and low.

They danced in and
out of the trees and
fluttered from flower
to flower.

"Look at me!" cried Abigail
as she skimmed the starry pond.

They swooped and looped and soared.
"I love being a fairy!" Abigail said.

"It's much more fun with two," laughed Twinkle
happily. At last she had a real friend of her own.

Soon it was time for Abigail to go back to being a little girl. "Thank you for making my wish come true," she said to Twinkle.

"You've made my wish come true, too!" replied Twinkle.

"Come back soon," said Abigail with a sleepy yawn.

Twinkle promised. "Just put your next
lost tooth in this fairy pouch, and
I'll be back as quick as the moths in the
moonlight," she said.

And as she flew away, she whispered ...

"Sweet dreams, my fairy friend!"